THE AMAZING TRAVELS OF WANNABE AND THE QUEST FOR KINDNESS

Written and illustrated by

T. F. MARSH

Standard
PUBLISHING
Bringing The Word to Life™

Cincinnati, Ohio

Text and illustrations © 2006 T. F. Marsh. © 2006 Standard Publishing, Cincinnati, Ohio.
A division of Standex International Corporation. All rights reserved. Printed in Italy.
Project editor: Greg Holder. Cover and interior design: Robert Glover.
Scripture quotations taken from the *New American Standard Bible*®, Copyright © 1960, 1962, 1963, 1968, 1971, 1972, 1973, 1975, 1977, 1995 by The Lockman Foundation.
Used by permission. (www.Lockman.org)
ISBN 0-7847-1802-4

12 11 10 09 08 07 06   9 8 7 6 5 4 3 2 1

The Bible says that we should be kind to one another. Now *that's* something this Wannabe would like to have—kindness!

I thought that kindness might be found high on a mountain, and with the Lord's help, I was sure I could find it. So I gathered my mountain gear and walking stick and headed up the mountain.

My quest began with a search on the ground. But I didn't find kindness hidden inside any rotten logs or buried underneath any dead leaves. (Yuck!)

Next I searched up high, near the sky. But I didn't find kindness stashed with the critters' acorns or tucked away in the woodpeckers' homes in the trees. Hmmm . . .

I'd know kindness when I found it, but where could it be?
I needed help to find it, and quick, because suddenly . . .

. . . a hungry grizzly bear growled at me, trying to shake a honey hive from my tree! I could have growled right back, but why not *help* him instead? He seemed very grateful. Hey, the Lord had shown me where it could be found—kindness!

Next, a cold and thirsty mountain man asked for a drink. A cup of hot chocolate would quickly do the trick. Looks like I found it again—kindness!

Moments later, two weary bighorn sheep wandered by looking for a place to rest. For these strangers, free room and board was waiting inside my tent. Kindness!

Then a freezing mountain lion shivered over my way. I knew just what to do! Wearing my extra set of clothes, he was toasty warm in no time. That's kindness!

From way up above me, I heard a sick little chick chirping loudly for help. After my daring rescue mission, the little bird was safely back in good hands. Now that's kindness!

Brrr! As I hiked higher up the mountain, the air grew colder. I stumbled upon snow bunnies trapped in an icy cave. Just the job for a superhero like me! That's kindness!

When I finally reached the mountaintop, there sat a grouchy, grumbling abominable snowman with a splinter in his finger. Even someone like him needs help now and then. That's kindness!

And then kindness was put to the test. An avalanche of snow thundered down the icy mountain! I was in danger but my friends were in trouble! Would I help them?

Yep, in a narrow escape, my friends and I made it down the mountain safe and sound.

You know, the Bible is right. The Lord does have kindness for those in need and he helped me to find it and act on it . . .

Greetings fellow traveler,

When I started on my adventure,
I thought that Kindness might be
found somewhere high in the mountains.
But I soon discovered that the Lord put Kindness in
my **heart**. And he can put it in your heart, too!

Kindness is seeing the needs of others and taking the time to help.
When you have Kindness, you'll want to give to others, even those who
can't pay you back. You'll want to help those in need even if it means
giving up something important to you. The Lord has shown Kindness to
all of us, and he will enable us to show Kindness to everyone around us. *I*
wanna be the best Wannabe showing Kindness that I can. How about you?

And be kind to one another, tender-hearted, forgiving each other,
just as God in Christ also has forgiven you.
Ephesians 4:32